Gone with the Wind
Part 2

MARGARET MITCHELL

Level 4

Retold by John Escott
Series Editors: Andy Hopkins and Jocelyn Potter

Pearson Education Limited
Edinburgh Gate, Harlow,
Essex CM20 2JE, England
and Associated Companies throughout the world.

ISBN-13: 978-0-582-41806-6
ISBN-10: 0-582-41806-2

Copyright © Margaret Mitchell 1936
First published in Great Britain by Macmillan London Ltd 1936
This adaptation first published by Penguin Books 1995
Published by Addison Wesley Longman Limited and Penguin Books Ltd. 1998
New edition first published 1999

7 9 10 8

Text copyright © John Escott 1995
Illustrations copyright © David Cuzik 1995
All rights reserved

The moral right of the adapter and of the illustrator has been asserted

Typeset by RefineCatch Limited, Bungay, Suffolk
Set in 11/14pt Monotype Bembo
Printed in China
SWTC/07

Published by Pearson Education Limited in association with
Penguin Books Ltd, both companies being subsidiaries of Pearson Plc

For a complet list of titles available in the Penguin Readers series please write to your local
Pearson Education office or contact: Penguin Readers Marketing Department,
Pearson Education, Edinburgh Gate, Harlow, Essex, CM20 2JE.

Contents

Introduction

'There is something left,' said Ashley. 'Something you love better than me. There's Tara!' And he pressed the wet earth into her hand.

Scarlett looked down, and suddenly she knew how very dear that red earth of Tara was to her – and how hard she would fight to keep it.

The war is over, and the Confederacy has lost. Scarlett has lost her husband and many friends in the fighting and she still cannot have the love of the man she really wants – Ashley Wilkes.

All she has is Tara, the home where she grew up, and now, when she has no money, even that may be taken away from her.

But Scarlett will do whatever she can to save Tara, even if she has to meet the terrible, dangerous Rhett Butler . . .

Gone with the Wind is the best-selling love story ever written. It has sold over twenty-eight million copies around the world since 1936, when it first appeared. It still sells two hundred and fifty thousand paperback copies every year in the United States alone.

The book made its writer, Margaret Mitchell, one of the best-loved writers in the world. When the film of *Gone with the Wind* was first shown in 1939, crowds waited for hours to see her. She was a beautiful woman. She was very funny, she enjoyed telling stories and she made people love to be with her – not unlike Scarlett O'Hara herself.

She was born in 1900 in Atlanta, Georgia. *Gone with the Wind* was written partly from the stories she heard as a child about the American Civil War and the old way of life in the Southern states. She spent ten years writing *Gone with the Wind*. It was the only book she ever wrote. She died in 1949, killed by a speeding car.

Chapter 1   Money Problems

On a cold January afternoon in 1868, Scarlett O'Hara was writing to Aunt Pitty when Will Benteen came into the room.

'Miss Scarlett,' he said, 'how much money do you have?'

She stared at him, wondering if something was wrong. 'I've got ten dollars in gold, the last of that Yankee's money.'

'That won't be enough for the taxes,' he said.

'Taxes?' said Scarlett. 'We've already paid the taxes.'

'Miss Scarlett, you don't go to Jonesboro often and I'm glad you don't,' he said. 'A lot of Yankees and Carpetbaggers★ are givin' the orders now.'

'But what's that got to do with our taxes?' said Scarlett.

'They're puttin' the value on Tara sky high and you'll have to pay more tax,' said Will. 'If you can't, Tara will be sold, and I've heard that somebody is hopin' to get it cheap.'

Will and Ashley looked after any business in Jonesboro, and had agreed not to tell Scarlett the more worrying details of what was happening. But Will could not hide this from her.

'Those Yankees!' she cried. 'Wasn't it enough for them to win the war? How much extra do they want us to pay?'

'Three hundred dollars,' said Will.

'Then we've got to get three hundred dollars somehow,' she said. 'They can't sell Tara!'

Will looked angry. 'They can and they'll enjoy doin' it. The country has gone to hell, if you'll excuse my sayin' so, Miss Scarlett. Carpetbaggers and white trash can vote, and most Southern gentlemen can't. Anyone who was on the tax books

★ Carpetbagger: a Northern white person who earned money from the building-up of the South during the time immediately after the American Civil War.

1

for more than two thousand before the war can't vote – men like your Pa and Mr Tarleton. I could vote if I took their Oath and became a Yankee, but I'll never do that! But people like Jonas Wilkerson and the Slatterys, *they* can vote, and they're givin' the orders now.'

'Vote!' cried Scarlett. 'It's taxes we're talking about. Will, we could borrow money on Tara and –'

'And who has any money to lend you on this place? Only the Carpetbaggers who are tryin' to take it away from you.'

'I've got the jewellery I took off the Yankee –'

'Miss Scarlett, who has money for jewellery round here?' said Will. 'Most people ain't got enough money to buy meat.'

They were silent for several minutes.

'Where is Mr Wilkes?' she said.

'He's in the field, cuttin' wood,' said Will.

Scarlett had not had a private talk with Ashley since his return because Melanie was always with him, but she found him alone in the field and told him the news.

'Only one person we know has money,' he said. 'That's Rhett Butler.' A letter from Aunt Pitty had said that Rhett Butler was back in Atlanta, looking rich.

'Don't talk about him,' said Scarlett. 'What about *us*?'

Ashley stared across the fields. 'What will happen to everybody in the South?' he said. 'I can't help, Scarlett. The world I belonged to has gone, and I'm afraid. I can't make you understand these things because you're never afraid. You face the real world without wanting to escape it, but I can't.'

'Escape!' cried Scarlett. 'Oh, Ashley, I do want to escape! I'm so tired of it all! Let's run away! We could go to Mexico – they want officers in the Mexican army. You know you don't love Melanie! You told me you loved me that day at Twelve Oaks, and I know you haven't changed.'

'We were going to forget that day at Twelve Oaks,' he said.

'You told me you loved me that day at Twelve Oaks, and I know you haven't changed.'

'Do you think I could ever forget it?' she said.

His voice was deadly quiet. 'And do you think I could leave Melanie and the baby? Scarlett, you're sick and tired, that's why you're talking this way. But I'm going to help you –'

'There's only one way to help me,' she said. 'Take me away. There's nothing to keep us here.'

'Only honour,' he said quietly.

She began to cry, and he took her into his arms and pressed her head against his chest, whispering, 'You mustn't cry.' And he kissed her, hungrily, as if he could never have enough.

'You do love me!' she cried. 'You do love me! Say it!'

He pushed her away. 'Don't!' he said. 'Or I shall make love to you now, here, in the field!'

She smiled, remembering the feel of his mouth on hers.

'We won't do this!' he cried. 'And it will never happen again, because I'll take Melanie and the baby and go!'

'Go?' she cried. 'Oh, no!'

'Yes, by God!' he said. 'Do you think I'll stay here now, when this might happen again?'

'But, Ashley you can't go. You love me!'

'All right, I love you! And a moment ago I almost took you, like a –' He could not find the words.

Scarlett felt a cold pain in her heart. 'If you felt like that and didn't take me, then you don't love me,' she said.

'I can never make you understand,' he said.

'There's nothing left for me to fight for,' she said.

He picked up some of the red earth at his feet. 'There is something left,' he said. 'Something you love better than me. There's Tara!' And he pressed the wet earth into her hand.

She looked down at it. And suddenly she knew how very dear that red earth of Tara was to her – and how hard she would fight to keep it.

'You needn't go,' she said. 'It won't happen again.'

4

Chapter 2   Return to Atlanta

Scarlett heard the sound of a horse and saw a shiny new carriage stop by the house. Jonas Wilkerson got out.

Scarlett was surprised to see the man who was once her father's plantation manager. Will had said that Jonas had made a lot of money – mostly by cheating negroes or the government – and here he was, stepping out of a fine carriage with a woman who was dressed in fashionable clothes. The woman looked towards the house, and Scarlett recognized her immediately.

'Emmie Slattery!' she said before she could stop herself.

'Yes, it's me,' said Emmie, holding her head proudly.

Emmie Slattery! That dirty, cheap female whose fatherless baby Scarlett's mother had helped to deliver! Emmie, who gave typhoid to Scarlett's mother and killed her. That overdressed, nasty piece of white trash was coming up the steps of Tara – smiling, and looking as if she belonged there!

'Get off those steps!' cried Scarlett. 'Get off this land!'

Jonas tried to control his anger. 'You mustn't speak like that to my wife,' he said.

'Wife?' said Scarlett. 'So you've made her your wife at last, have you?'

'We came to talk business with old friends –' began Jonas.

'Friends?' said Scarlett. 'My father threw you off this plantation after you fathered Emmie's baby. And the Slatterys took our help and paid us back by killing my mother. Get off this land before I call Mr Benteen and Mr Wilkes!'

Emmie ran back to the carriage, but Jonas did not move. 'Still the proud lady!' he shouted at Scarlett. 'Well, I know your father's gone crazy! And I know you can't pay your taxes. I came here to offer to buy this place, but I won't give you a dollar now! I'll buy it cheap when it's sold for taxes!'

'I'll pull this house down and plant every field with salt before either of you put a foot in it!' shouted Scarlett.

Jonas turned and walked angrily to the carriage. He climbed in next to his wife, who was crying, and they drove off.

Scarlett was so frightened that she found it difficult to breathe. Jonas Wilkerson at Tara? Never, never, never!

'I'll get money from Rhett!' she thought. 'I'll sell him the Yankee's jewellery, then I'll pay the taxes and laugh in Jonas Wilkerson's face!' Another thought came to her. 'But I'll need money for taxes every year.'

What had Rhett said?

'I want you more than I've ever wanted any woman.'

'I'll marry him,' she thought coolly, 'then I'll never have to worry about money again. But he mustn't suspect that we're poor or he'll know it's his money I want and not him.'

♦

Scarlett and Mammy stepped from the train at Atlanta. Scarlett had wanted to come alone, but Mammy wouldn't let her. And because Mammy had helped Scarlett make a new dress from some curtains, Scarlett felt unable to stop her coming.

Mammy knew about the taxes, and that they were in Atlanta to get the money to pay them. 'Why ain't you sayin' where the money is comin' from?' she asked, suspecting something. 'An' why do you need a new dress to borrow it?'

Scarlett didn't answer. They walked to Aunt Pitty's house, saddened by the city's burned and blackened buildings. The streets were full of Yankee soldiers, or negroes who stared at Scarlett in an insulting way as she walked past.

A closed carriage came along Peachtree Street and a woman's head appeared at a window. It was Belle Watling.

'Who was that?' asked Mammy. 'I ain't never seen hair that colour in my life!'

'She's the town's bad woman,' said Scarlett.

And Mammy's mouth fell open.

♦

'My dear, did I tell you that Rhett Butler was in prison?' Aunt Pitty said at supper that evening.

For a moment, Scarlett was so shocked she could only stare. 'Yes!' went on Aunt Pitty. 'He's in prison for killing a negro who insulted a white woman, and they may hang him!'

'How – how long will he be in prison?' asked Scarlett.

'Nobody knows,' said Aunt Pitty. 'And the Yankees don't care whether people are guilty or not, they're so worried about the Ku-Klux-Klan.* Do you have a Klan near Tara? I'm sure you do, and Ashley doesn't tell you about it. Klansmen aren't supposed to tell. They ride out at night, dressed like ghosts, and call on Carpetbaggers who steal and negroes who are rude or insulting. Sometimes they frighten them and make them leave. Sometimes they kill them and leave them with the Ku-Klux card on them. The Yankees are very angry about it, but I don't believe they'll hang Captain Butler because they think he knows where the money is. Everybody believes he's got millions of dollars in gold, belonging to the Confederacy. *Somebody* got it, and we think it was the blockaders.'

Millions – in gold! Scarlett imagined it. She could repair Tara, and plant miles and miles of cotton. She could have pretty

* Ku-Klux-Klan: a secret group of white people whose members punished others (often black people), for doing something which the Klan thought was a crime, even if the law didn't. They covered their faces and wore long white clothes.

7

clothes, and a good doctor to look after Pa. And Ashley – oh, she could do so much for Ashley!

Chapter 3   Prison Visiting

There were soldiers talking outside the Yankee prison. Scarlett, wearing her new dress, walked towards them.

'Can I help you?' one asked politely.

'I want to see Captain Butler,' said Scarlett.

'Butler again? That man's popular,' said the soldier. He was also a captain. 'Are you a relation?'

'Yes – his – his sister.'

The captain laughed. 'He's got a lot of sisters One of them was here yesterday. Come and wait in the office.'

Scarlett's face was red as she sat down on a chair and gave the soldier her name. After a time the door opened and Rhett appeared. He was dirty and hadn't shaved, but he came in with a smile and was obviously happy to see her.

'Scarlett!' he said, laughing. 'My dear little sister!'

He kissed her cheek before she could stop him.

'Remember, my men are just outside,' the captain said.

When the door closed after him, Rhett moved towards her again. 'Can I give you a real kiss now?' he said.

She smiled at him. 'Only on the cheek, like a good brother.'

'I'll wait and hope for better things,' he said. 'When did you arrive in Atlanta?'

'Yesterday,' she replied.

'And you came here this morning! My dear, how good of you!'

'Aunt Pitty told me about you last night and I just couldn't sleep, I was so unhappy and worried about you,' she said.

'Scarlett, it's wonderful to hear you say things like that,' he said. 'How pretty you are! Let me look at you.'

She laughed and turned round on her toes.

'What have you been doing since I last saw you?' he said.

She sat down next to him and put a hand on his arm. 'The Yankees came to Tara, but they didn't burn the house. Everything is fine. We did well with our cotton last autumn, and Pa says we'll do better next year, but there are no parties, Rhett, and I get bored in the country. I came here to get some dresses, and then I'm going to Charleston to visit my aunt.' She gently squeezed his arm. 'I'm so frightened for you, Rhett. They won't really hang you, will they?'

He put his hand on hers. 'Will you be sorry?' he said. 'If you're sorry enough, I'll put you in my will.' There was laughter in his eyes as he squeezed her hand.

His will! She looked down quickly, but not before he saw the excitement in her face. He watched her closely as he spoke.

'The Yankees think I ran away with the Confederacy gold.'

'Well – did you?' she said. 'Where *did* you get all your money? Aunt Pitty says –'

'What rude questions you ask!' he said, laughing.

She was so excited it was difficult to talk sweetly to him.

'You're too clever to let them hang you,' she said. 'You'll find a way to get out, and when you do –'

'And when I do –?' he asked, moving closer to her.

'Well, I –' Her face went prettily red again. 'Oh, Rhett, I'll die if they hang you. I –' She stopped and looked down.

'Scarlett, you can't mean that you –'

She tried to cry. Would tears seem more natural? She closed her eyes but turned her face upwards so that he could kiss her more easily. But he did not kiss her lips. He took her hand and kissed it, then turned it over to kiss the other side. It was rough from work, and the nails were broken. It wasn't the soft, white

9

hand of Scarlett O'Hara. He picked up the other one and looked at them together.

'Look at me!' he said, quietly. 'So everything is fine at Tara, is it? Well, these aren't the hands of a lady!'

'Don't say that!' she cried. But she was thinking, 'Why didn't I wear Aunt Pitty's gloves? How stupid!'

'You've worked like a field negro,' he said, dropping them. 'Why did you lie? I almost believed you were sorry for me.'

'But I *am* sorry,' she said.

'No, you aren't. You want something. Tell me what it is instead of behaving like a prostitute selling herself.' He looked closely at her. 'Did you really think I'd marry you?'

Her face went red.

'You know I'm not a marrying man,' he went on.

'Oh, Rhett, you can help me – if you'll just be sweet!'

'What do you want? Money?'

'Well – yes – I do want some money,' said Scarlett. 'I want you to lend me three hundred dollars.'

'You were talking about love but thinking about money,' he said. 'How like a woman! What will you offer me in return?'

'Jewellery?' she said.

'I'm not interested in jewellery,' he said.

'There's Tara –'

'No,' he said. 'What do you want the money for?'

'To pay taxes,' said Scarlett. 'Oh, Rhett, I lied about everything being all right. Pa is – not himself since Mother died. And there are thirteen of us to feed, and we never have enough to eat, or warm clothes or –'

'Where did you get the dress?' he asked.

'It's made out of some curtains,' she said.

He was silent for a moment, then he said, 'I don't like your first offer. Make me another one.'

She took a deep breath and looked him straight in the eye.

'You said you had never wanted a woman as much as you wanted me. Well – well, if you still want me, you can have me!'

He looked back at her and she felt her face getting hot. Then he said, 'Let me understand this: if I give you three hundred dollars, you will be my lover. Is that right?'

'Yes,' she said. 'Are you going to give me the money?'

He smiled. 'I couldn't give it to you. I have the money, yes, but not here. And I'm not saying where it is or how much.'

Her face became ugly and she jumped at him with an angry cry. He held her round the waist as she tried to bite and kick him.

'Let me go!' she said. 'You knew you weren't going to give me the money, but you let me go on! You're a hateful pig!'

He laughed. 'Come to my hanging, it will make you feel better,' he said.

'Thank you,' she said, 'but they may not hang you until it's too late to pay the taxes!'

Chapter 4   Another Plan

It was raining when she started to walk back to Aunt Pitty's house. Her clothes were soon wet, but she didn't care. 'How can I go back to Tara and tell them they must all go – somewhere?' she thought. 'Oh, I hope they hang Rhett Butler!'

She heard the sound of a carriage and turned to look.

The driver saw her. 'Is it – Miss Scarlett?' he said.

'Oh, Mr Kennedy!' said Scarlett. 'I'm so glad to see you!'

Frank Kennedy smiled and looked pleased as he stopped and helped her into the carriage. 'What are you doing in this part of the town?' he said. 'Don't you know it's dangerous?'

Scarlett noticed how well-dressed he was. The carriage was new, too. 'I didn't know you were here in Atlanta,' she said.

'Didn't Miss Suellen tell you about my shop?' said Frank.

'No,' she replied, although she remembered Suellen did say something about it. 'A shop? How clever you must be.'

'I came to Atlanta at the end of the war,' he explained, 'and there were beds and blankets on the train which nobody seemed to want. The Yankees were going to burn them but I got them first. I had ten dollars, and used it to put a roof on an old shop near Five Points, and I moved the beds and blankets in and started selling them. I sold them cheap, then bought other things and sold those, too.' He looked proud. 'I made a thousand dollars this year, Miss Scarlett. Five hundred went to buy more things, but I'll probably make two thousand next year, and I've already got an idea for another business.'

Scarlett quickly became interested. 'You have?' she said.

He laughed and hurried the horse along. 'A pretty little woman like you doesn't want to hear anything about business.'

'The old fool!' she thought, but she said, 'Oh, but I *do*,' and smiled sweetly. 'What other business?'

'A sawmill,' he said. 'I haven't bought it yet, but I will. Anybody who owns a sawmill can make money. The Yankees burned so many houses, and people have gone crazy building new ones. They can't get enough wood, and they can't get it fast enough. I'm going to buy this sawmill as soon as people pay me some of the money they owe me.' His face went red again. 'You know *why* I want to make money quickly, don't you?'

Scarlett knew he was thinking of Suellen. For a moment, she wondered about asking him to lend her three hundred dollars. 'But he won't,' she thought. 'He wants to marry Suellen in the spring, and if he lends me the money the wedding will have to wait. Oh, why does this old fool want to marry her? Once she gets her hands on his money, she won't care whether Tara is sold for taxes or burned to the ground!' Suddenly, an idea came into her head. 'Can I make him forget Suellen and ask *me* to marry him instead? He's old enough to be my father. But he's a gentleman, and now isn't the time for me to be fussy.'

He saw her staring at him and she looked away quickly.

'Are you cold?' he asked.

'Yes,' she said, in a small voice. 'May I put my hand in your coat pocket? I forgot to bring my gloves.'

'Oh – of course!' he said, delighted. 'But why did you come to this part of town?'

'I – I went to see if the soldiers would buy some clothes I had made to send home to their wives,' she lied.

'You went to the Yankees?' he said, shocked. 'Miss Scarlett! Does Miss Pittypat know that you –?'

'Oh, I shall *die* if you tell Aunt Pitty!' said Scarlett, and began to cry. It was easy to cry because she was so cold.

Frank became embarrassed. He wanted to put her head on his shoulder, but didn't know what to do.

'I came to Alanta to try to make a little money for myself and my son,' said Scarlett, tears running down her cheeks.

And then Frank saw that her head *was* on his shoulder, although he didn't know how it had got there.

'I won't tell Miss Pittypat,' he said, 'but you must promise not to do anything like this again.'

Her green eyes looked up at him. 'But I must do something. There's nobody to look after me or my poor little boy now.'

'There will always be a home for you and Wade with us when Miss Suellen and I are married,' he said.

Scarlett tried to look embarrassed.

'Is something wrong?' said Frank.

'I – I thought she wrote to you,' said Scarlett. 'Oh, she should be ashamed! Oh, what an unkind sister I have!'

Frank stared at her, his face grey. 'What –?'

'She's going to marry Tony Fontaine next month,' lied Scarlett. 'She got tired of waiting for you.'

♦

During the next two weeks, Scarlett made him feel like a strong, warm-hearted man who was lucky enough to catch a charming but helpless little woman. And when they stood together to be married, he still did not know how it had all happened. And so quickly too! He only knew that for the first time in his life he had done something wonderful and exciting.

No friends or relations came to the wedding. That was how Scarlett wanted it. 'Just us two, Frank,' she said. 'I always wanted to run away and be married. Please, dear, just for me!'

And before he knew it, he was married!

Chapter 5   The Sawmill Business

Frank gave Scarlett the three hundred dollars, although it ended his hopes of buying the sawmill. But she let him see how happy this made her, and then he was happy, too.

Will wrote to say the taxes were now paid and that Jonas Wilkerson was angry not to get Tara. Scarlett knew that Will understood why she had married Frank, but wondered what Ashley thought of her. She also had a letter from Suellen. A violent, insulting letter. And though many of the things Suellen said were true, Scarlett never forgave her for saying them.

She knew people in Atlanta were talking about her, but she did not care. Tara was safe. Now she had to make Frank realize that his shop must bring in more money. There were next year's taxes to pay – and there was still the sawmill. Scarlett knew that there was money to be made from the sawmill.

Nobody knew just when Frank realized that Scarlett had

tricked him into marrying her. Suellen certainly never wrote to tell him. Perhaps it was when Tony Fontaine came to Atlanta on business, obviously not married. But Frank could not believe Scarlett had married him coldly and without *any* love.

Two weeks after the wedding he became ill, and Dr Meade sent him to bed. As each day passed, Frank worried more and more about the shop, and the boy who was looking after it for him.

'I'll go and see how things are,' Scarlett told him.

When she arrived, she sent the boy out for his dinner then looked at the books to see just how much money people owed Frank. She was shocked to find it was more than five hundred dollars! And owed by people she knew — the Elsings and the Merriwethers, among others.

'Frank may be willing to stay poor just to be friendly with these people,' she thought, 'but I'm not!'

She was making a list of the names when the door opened and someone came in. It was Rhett Butler.

'My dear Mrs Kennedy,' he said. 'My *very* dear Mrs Kennedy!'

She stared at him. 'What are you doing here?' she said.

'I heard you were married, so I came to congratulate you.'

'Oh, you are the most —! What a pity they didn't hang you!'

'There are others who share your opinion,' he said, smiling.

'How did you get out of prison?' she asked.

'I persuaded a government friend of mine in Washington to speak for me,' he said. 'I knew things about him that he didn't want others to know.'

'But you were guilty,' she said.

'Yes, I did kill the negro,' agreed Rhett. 'He insulted a lady.' He spoke softly. 'And don't tell Miss Pittypat but, yes, I do have the money, safe in a bank in England.'

'The money?' said Scarlett. 'You have the Confederate gold?'

'Not all of it!' he said, laughing. 'There must be fifty or more

15

blockaders who have some. But I've got nearly half a million! If only you had waited and not rushed to marry again!'

Scarlett felt sick. Half a million dollars. It was hard to believe there was so much money in this cruel world.

'Tell me,' he said, trying not to look too interested, but failing, 'did you get the money for the taxes?'

And suddenly, she knew that *this* was why he was here. It was not to laugh at her, but to make sure she had got the money to pay the taxes. Oh, how nice he could be sometimes! Did he really care about her, more than he was willing to say?

'Yes, I got the money,' she said.

'Did you wait until you had the wedding ring on your finger?' he said, smiling 'And did Frank have as much money as he told you, or did he trick you? You needn't have secrets from me, Scarlett. I know the worst about you.'

'Oh, Rhett, you're the worst – well, I don't know what! No, Frank didn't trick me but –' Suddenly it was good to tell someone her troubles. 'Rhett, if Frank would just ask people for the money they owe him, I wouldn't be worried.'

'Don't you have enough to live on?' he said.

'Yes, but – well, I *could* use a little money.'

'I'll lend you some money, but I want to know what it's for,' said Rhett. He smiled again. 'And I won't ask you to repeat that charming offer you made me once.'

'You're a –!' she began.

'I know you're worrying about that,' he went on, smoothly. 'Not worrying a *lot*, but worrying a little. Now, why do you want money? Not for Ashley Wilkes, I hope.'

She became hot with anger. 'Ashley Wilkes has never taken a dollar from me! Ashley is –'

'Oh, yes!' he said. 'Ashley is wonderful! So why doesn't he take his family and get out of Tara, and find work?'

'He's been working like a field negro! He's –'

'Yes, he does the best he can, but you'll never make a farm worker out of a Wilkes. Now, cool down and tell me how much money you want, and what you want it for.'

Scarlett tried to control her anger. She wanted to throw his offer back in his face, but she told herself to be sensible.

'I want to buy a sawmill,' she said at last, 'and I think I can get it cheap. And I want two wagons and horses, and a horse and carriage for myself.'

'A sawmill?' said Rhett.

'Yes,' she said. 'Are you busy this afternoon?'

'Why?' he asked.

'I want you to drive to the sawmill with me,' she said. 'I want to buy it before you change your mind!'

♦

'The sawmill?' cried Frank. 'You sold your jewellery to Captain Butler and bought the sawmill?'

It was the shock of Frank's life when Scarlett told him. At first he thought she was joking, but he soon discovered that it was no joke.

Early each morning she drove out to the sawmill with Uncle Peter, Aunt Pitty's old slave, and did not come back until it was dark. A man called Johnson was made manager and he brought in free negroes to do the work. And Scarlett was soon earning enough money to talk about buying another sawmill.

Frank couldn't understand it. This wasn't the soft, sweet, help-less person he had married. This Scarlett knew what she wanted, and went after it – like a man! And she became angry so easily. He only had to say, 'Scarlett, I wish you wouldn't –' and it was like a thunder-storm breaking!

'A baby,' he thought. 'She needs a baby.'

Then, on a wild wet night in April, Tony Fontaine rode in from Jonesboro and knocked on their door, waking up Frank and Scarlett. Frank hurried down to let him in. Scarlett followed moments later, and came downstairs as Tony blew out the lighted candle Frank was holding.

'They'll hang me if they catch me!' Tony was saying. 'I'm going to Texas to hide, but I need another horse, Frank.'

'You can have mine,' said Frank.

'What happened?' Scarlett asked.

'You remember Eustis, who was one of our slaves?' said Tony. 'He came to the kitchen today, while Sally was making dinner. I don't know what he said but I heard her scream and try to get away. I ran into the kitchen, and there he was – drunk.'

'Go on,' said Scarlett.

'I shot him, and when Mother ran in to look after Sally, I began riding into Jonesboro to find Jonas Wilkerson. *He* was to blame. He had talked to those black fools and told them that negroes could have anything – could have white women!'

'Oh, Tony, no!' cried Scarlett.

'Yes!' said Tony. 'On my way past Tara I met Ashley and he went with me. We found Wilkerson in a bar, and I took my knife to him while Ashley held the others back. It was finished before I knew it. Wilkerson was dead and Ashley was putting me on my horse and telling me to come to you. He's a good man, Ashley.'

'But surely if you went back and explained –'

Tony laughed. 'Scarlett, how do you think the Yankees will reward a man for keeping negroes off his women? By hanging him, that's how! Now, I must go.'

Scarlett was afraid. Someone could rape or kill her, and the Yankees would hang anyone who tried to punish the criminal. She didn't want her children to grow up with all this hate and fear. She wanted them to know only warm homes, good clothes and fine food.

'Only money can buy these things,' she thought. 'Lots of money. That's what I'll have, and I don't care how I get it!'

Scarlett followed moments later, and came downstairs as Tony blew out the lighted candle Frank was holding.

When Tony had gone, Scarlett told her husband a secret she had kept for several weeks.

'Frank,' she said, 'I'm going to have a baby.'

♦

The spring months went by, and each day Scarlett went to the sawmill, certain that Johnson the manager was cheating her but unable to catch him. And she went to see builders and people who were planning new homes. She often lied about the quality of her wood, and sold bad wood for the same price as good wood.

One man who owned another sawmill openly called her a liar and a cheat, but it hurt his business because people would not believe that someone like Scarlett – a lady – would behave the way this man was saying she did. In the end, the man had to sell his business – and Scarlett bought it cheap.

She had to find someone to manage the second sawmill and she gave the job to Hugh Elsing. He was not a good businessman, but he was honest.

People were shocked to see Scarlett doing business with Yankees. But Scarlett did not care. 'When I'm rich,' she thought, 'I'll say what I think of them, but until then I'll smile sweetly and take their money.'

Then in early June, a message came from Will at Tara. Gerald, Scarlett's father, was dead.

Chapter 6   Changes at Tara

It was evening when Scarlett arrived in Jonesboro. Will met her with the wagon and they drove along the road towards Tara.

'Scarlett, I'm goin' to marry Suellen,' he said.

'Suellen!' she said. 'I always thought you loved Careen.'

'The only man Careen loved – that Tarleton boy – was killed in the war. And now she's goin' into the church in Charleston to live an' work.'

'Are you joking?' said Scarlett.

'No, and you mustn't argue with her or laugh at her,' he said. 'It's all she wants now. Her heart is broken.'

'But you don't love Suellen, do you?' she said.

'I do, in a way,' he said. 'And Ashley and Melanie will be goin' soon, and I couldn't live at Tara then without marryin' Suellen. You know how people talk –'

'Ashley?' said Scarlett. 'Going where?'

'Up North,' said Will. 'A Yankee friend wrote to him about workin' in a bank there.' He looked at her, and she had the old feeling that he knew all about her and Ashley.

'He can't go!' she thought. 'I'll find him a job at the sawmill, but he must think he's helping me or he won't come.'

'Tell me about Pa,' she said.

'He wasn't ill,' said Will, 'but – well – about a month ago Suellen talked to some people in Jonesboro, and afterwards she was all excited, although she didn't say anythin'. Then she started goin' for walks with your Pa. I saw her talkin' to him, but I'm sure he didn't know what she was sayin' half of the time. But now I know that she was tryin' to make him take the Yankee Oath.'

'Pa take the Yankee Oath!' cried Scarlett.

Will nodded. 'So that the Yankees would pay $150,000 for the cotton they burned at Tara during the war. They'll do that for any Southern gentleman who takes the Oath.'

'$150,000!' said Scarlett. And all for signing a loyal Oath to the United States Government. That much money for a small lie! Scarlett didn't blame Suellen.

'Well, Suellen got your father drunk and took him into Jonesboro, and he almost signed it,' Will went on. 'But at the last

21

moment he realized what he was doing and he threw the paper in Suellen's face. Then he rode off like a crazy man.'

'Oh, poor Pa,' said Scarlett.

'That evening, Ashley and I heard him riding across the fields,' said Will. 'He tried to jump the fence. "Look, Ellen! Watch me jump this one!" he shouted. But the horse stopped, and threw him over. The fall broke his neck.'

◆

Gerald O'Hara's funeral was on a hot June morning. People said kind words to Scarlett and Careen, but they did not speak to Suellen. She had tried to make her father forget his honour as a loyal Southerner and take the Yankee Oath, and they would never forgive her for that.

When everyone had gone after the funeral, Scarlett asked Ashley to speak with her. When they were alone, she offered to make him a half owner in one of her sawmills in Atlanta.

'Ashley, you must come,' she said. 'It may be months before I can look after the sawmills now, because of the baby –'

'Scarlett! Please!' he said. 'I can't –!'

'But you'll go to New York and live with Yankees!' she said.

'Yes,' he said. 'I've decided to go North. I've taken too much from you already, Scarlett – food, a home, clothes for myself and Melanie and the baby. And I can't – you know I can't live near you, and you know why.'

'Oh – that?' she said. 'I made a promise out in the field last winter, and I'll keep it.'

'I can't be sure I will,' he said. 'I'm going to New York.'

'Oh, Ashley!' said Scarlett, and began to cry wildly.

Moments later, Melanie came in, her eyes wide with worry. 'Scarlett, what is it? Is it the baby –?'

'It's Ashley – he's so – so horrible!' shouted Scarlett.

'Ashley, what have you done?' Melanie ran to Scarlett.

'Let me explain,' said Ashley. 'Scarlett was kind enough to offer to make me manager of one of her sawmills in Atlanta.'

'Manager!' cried Scarlett, angrily. 'I offered to make him half-owner and he –'

'I told her I had arranged for us to go North and she –'

'Oh!' Scarlett began to cry again. 'I told him how much I need him – how I can't get anybody to manage the sawmill – and he refused to come! And now I'll have to sell it and we'll probably all go hungry, but he won't care!'

'Ashley, how could you refuse?' cried Melanie. 'After all Scarlett has done for us! She saved my life in Atlanta when my baby came. And she killed a Yankee here, to save us. Yes, did you know that? And now, the first time she asks us to do some-thing for her –! Oh, Ashley, just think what it will mean for us to live in Atlanta among our own people. Maybe we'll have a little home of our own. Oh, Ashley, do say yes!'

Scarlett looked into Ashley's tired eyes as he spoke.

'I'll come, Scarlett,' he said. 'I cannot fight you both.'

Chapter 7   Danger in Atlanta

Scarlett was disappointed when Ashley was not a better businessman than Hugh Elsing. But she could do nothing about it until after her baby was born.

'I'll never have another child!' she decided.

Scarlett's baby was a girl – Ella – and she was born during a week when a negro raped a white woman and was quietly hanged by the Ku-Klux-Klan before he could be brought to the law. Scarlett thanked God that Ashley was too sensible to belong to the Klan, and that Frank was too old and weak.

But people stayed at home behind locked doors, and men were afraid to leave their women and children unguarded. Both

Ashley and Hugh stayed at home, and work at the sawmills stopped, which annoyed Scarlett. After three weeks, she got up from her bed and said that she was going to the sawmills again. Frank and Mammy said it was too dangerous, so Scarlett rushed across to Ashley's house, which was at the bottom of Aunt Pitty's garden, and complained loudly to Melanie.

'I *will* go,' she said. 'I'll carry a gun and shoot anybody who tries to hurt me.'

Melanie was shocked. 'Scarlett, I'll die if anything happens to you! I'll tell Ashley to go back to the sawmill at once.'

'What good will he be if he's worried about you every minute of the day?' said Scarlett. 'No, I'll walk there and get some negro workmen on the way –'

'No!' said Melanie. 'Decatur Road is full of bad negroes, and you'll have to pass by there. I'll think of something.'

And that afternoon, a tall, thin old man with a wooden leg and only one eye came across the garden from Melanie's house. He was one of the many old soldiers without homes or families who stopped at Melanie's house and were given food and a place to sleep before moving on again.

'Mrs Wilkes sent me to drive for you,' he said. 'My name's Archie, and Mrs Wilkes has been good to me, so here I am.'

Scarlett didn't like the look of him, but she said, 'All right. If my husband agrees.'

Frank was disappointed when the baby did not change Scarlett, but she was determined to go to her sawmills, so he agreed to let Archie drive her.

Scarlett sometimes wondered about Archie's earlier life and, one morning, she learned something about it.

'You can never be sure that free negroes will come to work,' she was saying. 'I'm going to get some convicts.'

Archie turned to her angrily. 'The day you get convicts at the sawmills will be the day I stop workin' for you. People who use convicts don't care. They feed them cheaply and get all the work they can out of them.'

'Why do you care?' she said.

'Because *I* was a convict for nearly forty years,' he said.

A shocked Scarlett listened to his story. Archie murdered his wife because she was his brother's lover, and he was sent to prison for the rest of his life. But during the war, when things were going badly for the Confederacy, convicts were given the chance to go free if they fought against the Yankees. Archie took his chance and was now a free man.

'Mrs Wilkes knows,' said Archie. 'I wouldn't let a nice lady like her take me into her house without knowin'.'

Scarlett said nothing, but she thought, 'A murderer! How could Melanie be so – so –? Oh, there are no words for it.'

But when she began using convicts – five for each sawmill – Archie kept his promise and stopped driving her. Frank also asked Scarlett not to use convicts, and at first Ashley refused to work with them. But Scarlett got her own way eventually, although Ashley did no better with the convicts than he had with negroes. And now there were grey hairs in his head and a tired look in his eyes, and he almost never smiled.

♦

On a warm December day, Scarlett was sitting outside Aunt Pitty's house with her baby when she looked up to see Rhett Butler riding along the road.

'Hello, Rhett,' she said. 'You've been away a long time.'

'Yes, I have,' he said. 'And I was on my way to see you when I saw Mrs Ashley Wilkes. It was quite a surprise. Of course, I stopped to talk with her, and she told me that you were kind enough to make Mr Wilkes a half-owner in your sawmill.'

'What about it?' said Scarlett, looking guilty.

'When I lent you that money, you promised not to use it to look after Ashley,' he said. 'Scarlett, you have no honour.'

'Why do you hate Ashley?' she said.

'I don't, I pity him. His world is gone and he's like a fish out of water. How did you get him to come to Atlanta?'

Scarlett pushed the memory of the argument with Ashley from her mind. 'I explained that I needed his help because I was going to have a baby. He was pleased to come.'

'Well, you'll never get another dollar out of me,' said Rhett. He looked down at the baby. 'I suppose Frank is very proud of his daughter and has lots of plans for her.'

'Yes, well, you know how silly men are with their babies.'

'Then tell him to stay home at night more often, if he wants to see her grown up,' said Rhett.

'What do you mean?' said Scarlett. 'Are you trying to tell me that Frank is – is –? Oh!'

Rhett laughed loudly. 'I didn't mean he was seeing other women! Frank? Oh, how funny!' And he went away laughing.

Chapter 8   Ku-Klux-Klan

The March afternoon was cold as Scarlett drove alone along the Decatur road. Frank's gun was on the seat beside her as she went past old army tents and rough wooden buildings where the black prostitutes, and the white and negro criminals lived.

Suddenly, a big negro stepped out from behind a tree.

Scarlett quickly picked up Frank's gun. 'What do you want?'

'Miss Scarlett! Don't shoot Big Sam!' came the reply.

Big Sam! He was one of the slaves who had worked at Tara and who went to fight for the Confederacy in the last months of the war. 'Sam!' said Scarlett. 'What are you doing in this nasty place? And why haven't you been into town to see me?'

'I don't live here, Miss Scarlett,' said Sam. 'I'm just stayin' here for a time. I went up North, but I didn't like it, an' I'm goin' home to Tara as soon as I get the chance.'

'Would you like to stay here and work for me?' said Scarlett. 'I need a driver.'

Sam looked unhappy. 'Thank you for offerin', Miss Scarlett, but I've got to get out of Atlanta. I – I killed a man.'

'A negro?'

'No, a white man. A Yankee soldier,' said Sam. 'He said somethin' bad an' – I didn't mean to kill him, but I'm strong, an' – an' now they're after me!'

Scarlett thought for a moment, then said, 'I'll send you to Tara tonight. I have to drive out to my sawmill now, but I'll be back before it's dark. Wait for me here.'

'Yes, Miss Scarlett,' said Sam. Like many 'free' negroes, he was pleased to have somebody to tell him what to do again.

That evening, the sun had gone when Scarlett reached the bend in the road. Big Sam was nowhere to be seen, and she began to worry. Then she heard feet coming along the road.

But it wasn't Sam. It was a big white man and a small, fat negro. Scarlett put her hand on the gun at her side.

'Lady, can you give me any money?' said the white man. He stopped Scarlett's horse and held it. 'I'm hungry.'

'Get out of the way,' she answered, keeping her voice calm.

'Get her!' the man shouted to the negro. 'She's probably got her money inside her dress!'

What happened next was like a terrible dream. The negro ran to the carriage and Scarlett shot at him, but the gun was pulled from her hand so roughly that it almost broke her wrist. Then she felt a hand at her throat, and her dress was torn open from her neck to her waist. The black hand pushed between her breasts, and Scarlett screamed like a mad woman.

'Shut her up!' shouted the white man. 'Pull her out!'

Then the negro jumped down as Big Sam came towards him.
'Run, Miss Scarlett!' shouted Big Sam

A third man was in the road and the white man suddenly cried out. Then the negro jumped down as Big Sam came towards him.

'Run, Miss Scarlett!' shouted Big Sam.

Scarlett started the horse and felt the carriage go over the white man, who was lying where Sam had knocked him down. Then she heard another shout from behind, and looked back to see Big Sam running after her. She slowed enough to let Sam jump on to the carriage, then rushed on towards the town.

♦

That night, Frank sent Big Sam to catch the train to Jonesboro. Then he took Scarlett, Aunt Pitty and the children to Melanie's and went off with Ashley.

Scarlett almost burst with anger. How *could* he go out tonight? The women were sitting together in Melanie's room. India, Melanie's cousin, was with them, and Archie was standing by the fire.

Scarlett wanted to scream. How could they be so calm? Did nobody *care*? But there was a nervousness about Melanie and India, she noticed. At each sound of a horse outside, they lifted their heads from their reading and looked at each other.

'Something's wrong,' thought Scarlett. 'But what is it?'

Then Archie said, 'Somebody's comin', and it isn't Mr Wilkes.' He moved to the door. 'Who's there?'

'Captain Butler,' came the answer. 'Let me in.'

Melanie ran to the door and pulled it open.

'Where have they gone?' Rhett said. 'Tell me quickly!'

'What's happened?' said Melanie. 'How – how did you know?'

'The Yankees have suspected them from the beginning, Mrs Wilkes,' said Rhett. 'They knew there was going to be trouble tonight, and they've prepared for it. I heard two Yankee officers talking about it. Your husband and the others will be caught. Where did they go? Have they got a meeting-place?'

'Don't tell him!' shouted Archie. 'It's a trick. Didn't you hear him say he was with Yankee officers?'

But Melanie was looking at Rhett. Her voice shook as she spoke to him. 'Out on the Decatur road,' she said. 'They meet at the old Sullivan plantation – the one that's half- burned.'

'Thank you,' said Rhett. 'I'll ride fast. When the Yankees come, pretend you know nothing.' He went out into the black night, and they heard him ride away at great speed.

Aunt Pitty gave a cry. 'The Yankees – coming here?'

'What's it all about?' said Scarlett. 'What does it mean?'

'Mean?' said India. 'It means you've probably caused Ashley's and Mr Kennedy's deaths!'

'Where's Ashley?' cried Scarlett. 'What's happened to him?'

'Where's your *husband*?' said India, her eyes full of anger. 'Aren't you interested in him?'

'India, please!' said Melanie, her face white and shocked. 'Scarlett, we didn't tell you because Frank thought – well, you were always against the Klan, and –'

'The Klan!' screamed Scarlett. 'Ashley? Frank?'

'Of course they are in the Klan!' said India. 'And all the other men we know. They are white men and Southerners!'

'Oh, now the Yankees will take my sawmills and the shop, and put Frank in prison!' cried Scarlett. She looked at them. 'What did Rhett Butler mean?'

India and Melanie were too afraid to speak.

'Mr Wilkes and Mr Kennedy and the other men have gone out tonight to kill that negro and that white man,' said Archie. 'Now its seems that the Yankees suspect somethin' and have sent soldiers to wait for them. And it's all because of you!'

Suddenly, there was the sound of horses outside the house, followed by somebody knocking hard at the door.

'Archie, open the door,' Melanie said quietly and calmly.

A Yankee captain and some soldiers stood outside. Scarlett recognized the captain. It was Tom Jaffery and he was a friend of Rhett's. He saw Scarlett and took off his hat.

'Good evening, Mrs Kennedy,' he said, looking round the room quickly. 'And which of you ladies is Mrs Wilkes?'

'I am,' said Melanie, coolly. 'Why are you here?'

'I'd like to speak to Mr Wilkes and Mr Kennedy,' he said.

'They aren't here. They're at Mr Kennedy's shop.'

'They're not at the shop,' he said, looking serious. 'We'll wait outside until they return.'

Soldiers surrounded the house, a man at each window and door. After a long time, there was the sound of horses feet – and of Rhett Butler singing! And there were other drunken shouts of 'What the hell!' from Ashley and Hugh Elsing.

Archie's hand moved towards his gun.

'No,' whispered Melanie firmly. 'I'll do this.' And she opened the door with an annoyed look on her face. 'Bring him in, Captain Butler,' she called. 'I suppose you've got him drunk again. Bring him in.'

The Yankee captain spoke from outside. 'I'm sorry, Mrs Wilkes, but I'll have to arrest your husband and Mr Elsing.'

'Arrest?' said Melanie. 'If you arrest everyone who is drunk, captain, your prison will be full of Yankee soldiers! Bring him in, Captain Butler, if you can walk yourself.'

Ashley was white-faced and wearing Rhett's long coat. He was half-carried into the room by Rhett and Hugh. The Yankee captain followed them, half-amused but suspecting something, too.

'Oh, Ashley, I'm ashamed of you!' cried Melanie. 'Drunk! And out with a Yankee-loving Carpetbagger like Captain Butler! Archie, take him to his room and put him to bed, as usual.'

'Don't touch him,' said the captain. 'I am arresting him for his part in a Klan killing. A white man and a negro were killed out near the Decatur road tonight, and Mr Wilkes –'

'Tonight?' said Rhett. He began to laugh. 'Not tonight, Tom. These two have been with me since eight o'clock.'

'With you, Rhett?' The captain was confused now. 'Where?'

'I don't like to say.' Rhett looked at Melanie, then looked away quickly. 'I hate to say it in front of the ladies.'

'I want to know!' said Melanie. 'Where was my husband?'

'At – at Belle Watling's house,' said Rhett. 'He was there with Hugh and Frank Kennedy and Dr Meade and – oh, a lot of others. We had a party. A big party – drinks, girls –'

'At Belle Watling's? Oh!' Melanie put a hand to her breast – and appeared to faint.

'Now you've done it, Tom!' cried Rhett. 'There won't be a wife in Atlanta who will speak to her husband.'

'Rhett, I didn't know –' The captain looked embarrassed.

'Go and ask Belle if you don't believe me,' said Rhett.

'But – I've got to arrest these men!'

'I didn't know it was against the law to get drunk at Belle's house,' said Rhett. 'Tom, there are fifty witnesses to say that they were there.'

'There always are,' said the captain. 'Oh, I'll go, but I want to see them in the morning for questioning.'

The captain went out, and Hugh Elsing went with him. India quickly closed the door, and they pulled all the curtains while Ashley was taken into the bedroom and put on the bed. Rhett's coat was taken off him. Melanie was on her feet again and she began cutting off Ashley's shirt. It was covered in blood.

'He's hurt!' cried Scarlett.

'You fool!' said India. 'Did you think he was really drunk?'

Melanie put a towel against Ashley's shoulder to stop the blood. He opened his eyes and smiled weakly at her.

Rhett said, 'I'm sorry I had to say that Mr Wilkes and the others were at Belle Watling's house, Mrs Wilkes, but I had to think quickly, and I know Belle will be glad to lie for me. When I got out to the old Sullivan plantation, I saw that Mr Wilkes was hurt and could not ride far, so I took him, Dr Meade, Mr Merriwether, Hugh Elsing and all the others to Belle's. No one saw us. We went in through a private door at the back which is always locked.' He looked Melanie straight in the eye. 'But I have a key.'

Melanie became embarrassed, but Scarlett was thinking: 'So it's true! He lives with that awful Watling woman.'

Rhett looked at Archie as Melanie turned back to Ashley. 'Take my horse to the old Sullivan place,' Rhett said to him. 'The white Klan clothes are pushed down under the floor. Burn them. And there are two – men in the back room. Put them over the horse and take them to the field behind Belle's house. Put guns in their hands. Shoot both guns at once – it's got to look like an ordinary shooting. Do you understand?'

Archie nodded, then said, 'Him?'

'Yes,' Rhett answered quietly.

And Archie went out of the back door.

Something about those two last words made Scarlett say, 'Where's Frank?'

Rhett took her arm and led her into the next room. Only when they were alone did he say, 'Archie's carrying him to the field behind Belle's. He's dead. Shot through the head.'

Chapter 9   Atlanta's Most Unpopular Couple

Scarlett sat in her bedroom drinking brandy and feeling sorry for things that she had done. She wondered if everyone in the town thought that she had killed Frank. People at the funeral that day had been cool with her, but she didn't care.

Somebody knocked on the door downstairs and she heard Aunt Pitty open it. Then came the voice of Rhett Butler, and she knew that he was the one person she *did* want to see tonight.

'I'm going away tomorrow and will be away some time,' he was saying to Aunt Pitty. 'It's very important that I see her.'

'Oh, but I don't think – not today –' Aunt Pitty began.

Scarlett ran to the top of the stairs. 'I'll be down in a moment, Rhett!' she called, and saw Aunt Pitty's surprised and shocked face looking up at her.

They talked together in the library, behind closed doors. Scarlett did not want Aunt Pitty to know about her drinking, but it was almost the first thing Rhett noticed.

'Brandy,' he said. 'And you've been drinking a lot of it.'

'What if I have?' she said.

'It's a bad thing to drink alone, Scarlett,' said Rhett. 'What's the matter? It's more than just old Frank dying.'

'Oh, Rhett, I was wrong to marry Frank! He loved Suellen but I lied and told him she was going to marry Tony Fontaine.'

'So that's how it happened,' said Rhett. 'I often wondered. But he didn't *have* to marry you. Are you sorry you still own Tara, and that you aren't poor and hungry?'

'No!'

'No, of course you aren't,' said Rhett 'It's the brandy that's making you feel sorry for yourself.'

'How dare you –!' began Scarlett.

'I'm going to England, and I may be away for months.' He smiled. 'I still want you more than any other woman, Scarlett, and now Frank is gone I thought you ought to know it.'

'Oh!' she cried. 'You are the rudest –! And on the day of Frank's funeral! Will you please leave this house –'

'Listen,' he said calmly. 'I'm asking you to marry me.'

'Is this one of your bad jokes?' she said angrily.

'It's no joke,' he said. 'I'm afraid that if I wait until I come back, you'll be married to some other man who has a little money. I can't go on waiting to catch you between husbands, Scarlett.'

'But – but Rhett, I don't love you,' she said.

'That wasn't important when you married before,' he said. 'What's *really* stopping you? Tell me.'

Suddenly she thought of Ashley.

'*It's because of him that I don't want to marry again,*' she thought. '*I belong to Ashley – to Ashley and Tara – for ever.*'

She did not know that her thoughts brought a look of softness to her face which Rhett immediately understood.

He became angry. 'Scarlett O'Hara, you're a fool!'

And then his arms were round her and he was kissing her, softly at first, and then violently, so that before she knew it she was kissing him back.

'Stop – please – I'm faint,' she whispered after a moment.

'None of the fools you've known have kissed you like this, have they?' he said. 'Charles or Frank or your stupid Ashley? What did they know about you? I know you.' His mouth was on hers again. Then he said, 'Say yes! Say yes, or –'

She whispered 'Yes' and felt a sudden calm come over her.

He looked down at her. 'You mean it?'

'Yes,' she said again.

'Why?' he said, suddenly uncertain. 'Is it my money?'

'Rhett! What a question!'

'Don't try to sweet-talk me. I'm not Charles or Frank,' he said. 'Is it my money?'

'Well – money does help, you know,' she said. 'And I am fond of you, Rhett. But if I said I loved you I would be lying, and you would know it.'

He looked at her and laughed, but it was not a pleasant laugh.

35

'All right,' he said. 'What shall I bring you back from England? A ring? What kind do you want?'

'Oh, a diamond ring, Rhett!' said Scarlett. 'And buy a great big one!'

♦

The ring Rhett brought back from England was so large that it embarrassed Scarlett to wear it. But only when it was on her finger did she tell everyone that she was going to marry him.

They became Atlanta's most unpopular couple, except for Yankees and Carpetbaggers. Everyone blamed Scarlett for Frank's death, and for putting the lives of other men in danger. And they hated Rhett for using Belle Watling, a prostitute, to save their men from the Yankee prisons. They were sure he did it on purpose, just to embarrass them.

Only Melanie was loyal to Scarlett, and reminded people how Scarlett had helped her and her family when they had no home.

'Those of you who do not visit Scarlett,' she told the ladies of Atlanta, 'need never, never visit me!'

Rhett took Scarlett to New Orleans after they were married, and he kept her too busy to think of Ashley very often. But sometimes, when she lay in Rhett's arms with the moonlight shining across the bed, she thought how perfect life could be if only it was Ashley's arms that held her so closely.

They stayed at the National Hotel in Atlanta while a house was built for them. There were many 'new people' (as old Atlantians called them) staying there, also waiting for their homes to be completed, and Scarlett found them pleasant and exciting to be with. They were rich and well-dressed, and never talked about the war or 'hard-times'.

Her house was the biggest and most fashionable in Atlanta. Rhett gave her anything she wanted and listened to her talk about the shop, her sawmills, the convicts and the cost of feeding them, and gave her good, sensible advice. He never talked about having children, as Charles and Frank had done.

But then Scarlett learned that she was going to have another baby, and told the news to Rhett.

'I won't have it!' she screamed. 'A woman doesn't have to have children if she doesn't want them! There are things –'

'Scarlett, you haven't done anything!' he shouted. 'I don't care if you have one child or twenty, but I do care if you die.' He held her close. 'I don't want children any more than you do, but I don't want to hear any more foolish talk.'

◆

Scarlett's baby was named Eugenie Victoria, but Melanie called her Bonnie, and she was always called this afterwards.

◆

When Scarlett was able to visit the sawmills again, she found that Ashley's was not doing well.

'Ashley, you're too soft-hearted,' she said. 'You ought to get more work out of the convicts. They only have to tell you they're sick and they stay away from work! That's no way to make money. A couple of knocks with a stick will –'

'Scarlett! Stop!' cried Ashley. 'Don't you realize they are men – some of them sick and weak and – oh, my dear, when I see the way he's hardened you, you who were always so sweet –'

'Who has hardened me?'

'Rhett Butler. Everything he touches he poisons. I know he saved my life, and I'm grateful, but I wish it had been any man but him. And when I think of him touching you, I –'

'He's going to kiss me!' thought Scarlett, happily. But he stepped back, as if realizing he had said too much.

'I'm very sorry, Scarlett,' he said. 'I mustn't say these things. I have no excuse except – except – no excuse at all.'

All the way home in the carriage Scarlett thought of his words. No excuse at all – except that he loved her and did not want to think of her lying in Rhett's arms! Well, in future she would live without those arms! The idea pleased her. And it would mean that she would not have to have any more children.

But how could she let Ashley know what she'd done for him?

'I wish I could talk to Ashley as easily as I can talk to Rhett,' she thought. 'But I'll let him know somehow. Of course, it will be difficult telling Rhett I want separate bedrooms.'

But it was not as difficult as she thought.

He gave her a long, cool look when she told him. 'Scarlett,' he said, 'if you and your bed still held any charms for me, locked doors would not keep me away. But fortunately the world is full of beds – and most of the beds are full of women.'

'You mean you'll –?'

'Of course,' he said. 'It's surprising I haven't taken advantage of one of them before.'

'I shall lock my door every night!' said Scarlett.

'Why? If I wanted you, no lock could keep me out.'

Chapter 10   A Surprise Party

It was Ashley's birthday and Melanie was giving him a surprise party. Everyone knew except Ashley. That morning, Scarlett, Melanie, India and Aunt Pitty were getting things ready.

'If you're going to the sawmill,' Melanie asked Scarlett, 'can you keep Ashley busy until five o'clock? If he comes home earlier, he'll catch us finishing cakes or something.'

Scarlett was always happy to be alone with Ashley. 'Yes,' she said. But she saw India look quickly at her. 'She always looks strangely at me if I speak of Ashley,' thought Scarlett.

'Keep him there for as long as you can after five o'clock,' said

Melanie, 'then India will drive down in the carriage and pick him up. And, Scarlett, come early tonight.'

As Scarlett rode home, she thought: 'She wants me to come early, but she doesn't want me to welcome guests with her and India and Aunt Pitty. And I wanted to stand next to Ashley and welcome guests with him. Why wasn't I asked?'

Rhett knew the answer, and told her. 'A Yankee-lover welcoming people, when all those important Confederate-lovers are going to be there? Don't be silly, my dear. It's only because of loyal Melanie that you're invited at all.'

Scarlett dressed with more care than usual for her trip to the shop and the sawmill that afternoon, and Ashley was surprised to see her at the office. There was almost a smile on his face when he welcomed her.

'Scarlett!' he said. 'Why aren't you at my house helping Melanie to get ready for the surprise party?'

'Ashley!' cried Scarlett. 'You aren't supposed to know!'

'Oh, I'll be the most surprised man in Atlanta,' said Ashley, with laughter in his eyes.

'Who told you?' she asked.

'Almost every man who is invited, and who has ever had a surprise party given to him,' said Ashley, and Scarlett had to smile. He took her hands, spreading them wide so that he could look at her dress. 'Scarlett, you get prettier all the time.'

But as he touched her, she realized for the first time ever that it did not excite her. 'How strange!' she thought.

'I'll always remember you as you were on that day at Twelve Oaks,' he said. 'You were wearing a white dress covered with little green flowers, sitting under a tree with a dozen boys round you.' He dropped her hands, and the light went out of his eyes. 'We've come a long way since then, Scarlett. You've come straight and quick, but I've come slowly. And without you, and all you've done for me, I'd be nothing now.'

'Oh, Ashley, you sound so sad!' cried Scarlett.

'No, I'm not sad any more,' he said. 'I –'

He stopped, but suddenly Scarlett knew what he was thinking. 'You're not sad,' she thought. 'You've just lost hope.'

'Ashley, what do you want?' she asked him.

'I don't know,' he said. 'Perhaps I want the old days back again. The memory of them never seems to go away.'

His voice and the way he spoke brought those memories back to her, and it hurt to think of them. 'I like these days better,' she said, but did not look at him when she spoke.

He laughed softly, put his hand under her chin and lifted her face up to his. 'Oh, Scarlett, what a poor liar you are!'

He made her remember things she wanted to forget – the beauty, the charm of the old days. 'I mustn't let him make me look back,' she thought. 'It hurts too much. That's what's wrong with Ashley. He's afraid of the future, so he looks back. Oh, Ashley, my love, you mustn't look back!'

She remembered the Scarlett O'Hara who loved pretty dresses and charming young men. Without warning, tears came into her eyes and began to fall down her cheeks, and she looked up at Ashley like a small, lost child. He took her gently in his arms, pressed her head against his shoulder, and put his cheek next to hers. Like a loved friend but not a lover.

She heard the sound of someone outside, and suddenly he pushed himself away from her. She looked up at him, but he was not looking at her. He was looking over her shoulder.

She turned. And there stood India – her face white and her eyes filled with anger. Archie was with her, and with them stood Mrs Elsing.

♦

Scarlett never remembered how she got out of the office. Shame and fear hurried her home to her empty house. It was silent in the April sunshine. The negroes were at a funeral and the children were playing in Melanie's garden.

Melanie!

Melanie would hear of this. Scarlett went cold at the thought as she went up to her room. The news would be all over town by supper-time, and people would believe that she and Ashley were lovers. And it had been so innocent, so sweet!

Scarlett burst into tears when she thought of the hurt in Melanie's eyes when India told her. 'What will Melanie do?' she thought. 'Will she leave Ashley? And what will Rhett do?'

Scarlett pulled off her clothes and lay down on the bed.

'I won't think of it now, I'll think of it later.'

She heard the negroes come back later. Mammy knocked on her door but Scarlett sent her away, saying that she didn't want any supper. Then, after a long time, Rhett knocked on her door and she said, 'Come in.'

'Are you ready for the party?' he said. It was dark and she could not see his face.

'I – I have a bad head,' she said. 'I don't think I'll go.'

There was a long pause before he replied. 'What a cowardly little cat you are!' And his voice was hard and cruel.

He knew! She lay shaking, unable to speak.

He lit the candle next to her bed and looked down at her, and she saw that he was dressed in evening clothes.

'Get up,' he said. 'We're going to the party.'

'Oh, Rhett, I can't – I won't go until –'

'If you don't show your face tonight, you'll never be able to show it in this town as long as you live,' he told her. 'And I won't have a coward for a wife. Get your clothes on!'

◆

Lights were on in every room of Melanie's house and Scarlett could hear the music far up the street. Rhett held her arm roughly and walked with her to the door.

41

'I'll face them!' she thought. 'I don't care what they say, or what they think. Only Melanie – only Melanie!'

The music stopped as they entered, and the room slowly became silent. Scarlett lifted her chin and made herself smile. Then someone came hurrying through the crowd.

Melanie went immediately to Scarlett's side and put an arm round her waist. 'What a lovely dress, my dear,' she said in her small, clear voice. 'India couldn't come tonight. Will you welcome our guests with me?'

Chapter 11   Wonderful – and Wild

Rhett sent Scarlett home from the party alone, and she went to her room. Oh, how awful it had been! She could not forget Ashley's face, full of shame. 'Will he hate me now?' she thought. 'Now that Melanie's love has saved us both? Melanie, who will always believe we were innocent.'

Scarlett got herself ready for bed, then went downstairs to get herself a drink. There was a light in the dining-room.

'Rhett must have come in quietly and not gone to Belle Watling's,' she thought. 'I'll go without my brandy, then I won't have to see him. And I'll lock the door of my room.'

But the dining-room door opened and Rhett was standing there with a candle. 'Do come and have your drink, Mrs Butler,' he said. And she saw that he was very drunk.

'I don't want a drink. I heard a noise –'

'You heard nothing,' he said. 'Come here!'

Scarlett went down to the dining-room.

'Sit down,' he told her. Always before, life had seemed to be a joke to him, but now Scarlett saw that something mattered to him, and it mattered very much. He poured out a glass of brandy and put it in her hand. 'You're wondering if Miss Melanie knows

*But the dining-room door opened and Rhett was
standing there with a candle.*

all about you and Ashley. Well, someone told her, but she didn't believe it. I don't know what lie Ashley Wilkes told her – but any lie would do, for she loves him and she loves you.'

'If you weren't so drunk, I –'

'You locked me out of your bedroom because you didn't want me, or my children!' he shouted. 'And all the time you were wanting Ashley Wilkes! Oh, how that hurt!'

She drank her brandy and stood up. 'You don't understand Ashley or me, and you're jealous of something you can't understand.' She turned and walked towards the door but he came across the room and held her against the wall.

'I'm sorry for you, my pretty little fool,' he told her. 'If I was dead, and Miss Melanie was dead and you had Ashley, do you think you could be happy with him? Hell, no! You would never know what he was thinking about. You would never understand his books or his music. But we, my dear wife, understand each other. I loved you, and I *know* you – and I want you!' Suddenly, he lifted her off her feet and into his arms, and began to climb the stairs. 'And this is one night you will not turn me out of your room!'

She screamed, but he kissed her so violently that everything was pushed from her mind. And then her arms were round his neck and her lips were shaking under his.

◆

When Scarlett woke up the next morning, he was gone. But she remembered the wild and wonderful night.

Rhett did not appear for dinner, or for supper. And when a second day passed without news of him, she was disappointed and afraid. Had he been in an accident? After the second night, she decided to go to the police. But as she finished her breakfast in her room, she heard his feet on the stairs.

'Oh, hello,' he said, coming in.

'Where – where have you been?' she asked.

44

'Don't you know? I thought the whole town knew, after the police called at Belle's the night before last –'

'Belle's! You've been with that woman –?'

'Of course,' he said. 'I hope you didn't worry about me.'

'You went to her from me, after – after –'

'Oh that,' he said, carelessly. 'I'm sorry for the way I behaved at our last meeting, Scarlett. I was very drunk.'

She wanted to cry. 'He just used me when he was drunk, like he does the women in Belle's house!' she thought.

'Get out!' she told him.

'Don't worry, I'm going,' he said. 'I just came to say that I'm going to Charleston and New Orleans and – oh, a very long trip. I'm leaving today and I'm taking Bonnie with me. Get Prissy to pack her little things. I'll take Prissy, too.'

'You'll never take my child out of this house,' she said.

'My child too, Mrs Butler. Have her packed and ready in an hour, or what happened the other night will be nothing compared to what *will* happen,' he said, his voice cold.

He was gone for three months and, during that time, Scarlett learned that she was going to have another baby – the result of that wild night with Rhett which still filled her with shame! But for the first time, she was glad, because now she had the time and the money for a child.

Rhett returned without warning. One day Scarlett heard Bonnie cry 'Mother!' and hurried from her room to the top of the stairs, where Bonnie threw herself into Scarlett's arms.

Rhett was at the bottom. He looked up at her with his dark eyes, and suddenly she was just glad that he was home.

'Where's Mammy?' asked Bonnie, and Scarlett let her go.

She watched Rhett come up the stairs and wondered if he would kiss her, but he did not.

'You don't look well, Mrs Butler,' he said in a careless voice. 'Does this mean that you've missed me?'

45

It made her angry, this careless way of his. She hadn't wanted to tell him like this, but now the words rushed to her lips. 'It's because I'm going to have a baby!' she said.

He looked surprised, and moved towards her, as if he was going to put a hand on her arm. Scarlett turned away from him with hate in her eyes – and his face hardened.

'And who's the happy father?' he said coolly. 'Ashley?'

Her voice shook with anger. 'You know it's yours! But I don't want it any more than you do! No woman would want the baby of a man like *you*! I wish it was anybody's but yours!'

She stepped forward to tear his face with her finger-nails. But he moved to one side quickly. Scarlett missed him and fell – over and over – to the bottom of the stairs.

Chapter 12   A Secret Plan

Scarlett lost the baby and almost died. Every time Melanie came out of Scarlett's room, she saw Rhett sitting on his bed, his door wide open, watching his wife's room. And when at last she was able to tell him that Scarlett was better, he put his head in his hands and began to cry.

Melanie had never seen a man cry before and it frightened her, but she closed the door softly and went to him. And when she put her hand on his shoulder, his arms went round her, and before she knew it, she was sitting on the bed and he was sitting on the floor with his head on her knees.

He began to talk wildly, telling Melanie things that made her cheeks go hot with embarrassment. 'Captain Butler, you must not tell me these things!' she said.

'You don't understand,' he cried. 'She didn't want a baby. We hadn't slept together –'

'Captain Butler! You mustn't say –!'

'I was drunk, and I wanted to hurt her –'

Melanie looked at him. 'Is it possible that he heard and believed the terrible lie about Ashley and Scarlett, and was jealous?' she thought, suddenly. 'No, he's too sensible. He's drunk, and his mind is running wild.'

'You can't understand!' he said. 'You're too good to understand. I was crazy with jealousy! She doesn't love me, she never has. She loves –' He stopped as his drunken eyes met hers and he realized who he was talking to. 'If I told you, you wouldn't believe me, would you?'

'No,' said Melanie, softly. She began gently to smooth his hair. 'Don't cry, Captain Butler. She's going to get well.'

A month later, Rhett put Scarlett on the train to Jonesboro with Wade, Ella and Prissy. Then he rode to Melanie's house where she was sitting outside.

'Scarlett has gone to Tara?' she said.

'Yes,' he said, smiling. 'Tara will do her more good than all of Dr Meade's medicines. But I'm worried about her health because she tries to do too much.'

'Yes, she does,' agreed Melanie.

'That's why I want Mr Wilkes to buy her half in the sawmills,' said Rhett. 'I know she'll sell to him.'

'Oh!' said Melanie. 'That would be nice, but –'

'Miss Melanie, I want to lend you the money,' said Rhett.

'That's kind of you, but we may never be able to pay –'

'I don't want you to pay it back,' he said. 'I'll just be glad to know that Scarlett isn't making herself ill. The shop will be enough to keep her busy and happy. Do you understand?'

'Well – yes, but –' said Melanie, uncertainly.

'You want to buy your son a horse, don't you? And you want him to go to a good university, and to Europe?' he said.

'Oh, of course,' cried Melanie. 'But everyone is so poor.'

'Mr Wilkes could make a lot of money out of the sawmills one day,' said Rhett. 'Will you do it, to help Scarlett?'

'You know I'll do anything in the world for her,' said Melanie. 'She's done so much for me. But my husband –'

'If I send the money to Mr Wilkes without telling him who has sent it, will you see that he uses it to buy the sawmills?' said Rhett. 'It must be our secret.'

Melanie was silent for a moment. Then she said, 'Yes. And Scarlett's lucky to have a husband who is so nice to her!'

♦

Scarlett came back from Tara looking much healthier and full of news. She asked, 'Has anything happened here?'

'Ashley wanted to know if I thought you'd sell him your sawmill, and the half-part you have in his,' said Rhett.

Scarlett looked surprised. 'Where did Ashley get the money?'

'It seems that it came from someone he nursed with typhoid at Rock Island,' said Rhett. 'It came with an unsigned letter from Washington. Of course, I told him you wouldn't sell. I told him that you enjoyed telling other people what to do.'

'Let me look after my own business!' she said, angrily. 'And – and I *will* sell them to him!'

Until that moment, Scarlett had never intended to sell her sawmills, but Rhett made her angry by speaking about her that way, and to Ashley of all people! So that same night, she sold the sawmills. And then wished that she hadn't.

Chapter 13   Two Deaths

When Bonnie was four, Rhett bought her a horse and taught her to ride. The two of them were often seen riding together. Then

Rhett decided that the time had come for her to learn to jump, and he built a low gate in the back garden.

Bonnie jumped the low gate easily and Scarlett could not help laughing at Rhett, who looked so proud. After the first week of jumping, Bonnie wanted the gate to be higher.

'The horse's legs aren't long enough,' Rhett told her.

'They are! They are!' said Bonnie. 'I jumped Aunt Melanie's fence, and that's *very* high!'

'Oh, all right!' said Rhett, laughing. 'But if you fall off, don't blame me.'

He made the gate higher, and Bonnie called to her mother: 'Mother! Watch me jump this one!'

'I'm watching, dear,' said Scarlett, smiling.

Watch me jump this one!

There was something about those words . . . what was it? Scarlett looked at her small daughter as Bonnie rushed towards the gate, her blue eyes full of excitement. 'They're like Pa's eyes,' thought Scarlett.

And then she remembered! She heard her father's voice: 'Ellen! Watch me jump this one!'

'No!' cried Scarlett. 'No! Oh, Bonnie, stop!'

But there was the terrible sound of breaking wood, and a cry from Rhett. Then Scarlett saw the horse running off without its rider.

◆

Bonnie died from a broken neck. Three nights later, Mammy went to Melanie's house.

'Miss Melanie,' said Mammy. 'Mr Rhett won't let us take that poor child, an' there's the funeral tomorrow.'

'Won't let you take her?' said Melanie.

'He put her in his room and told me to bring lots of lights, and not to close the curtains. "Don't you know that Miss Bonnie is afraid of the dark?" he says. So I get him a dozen candles, an' he says "get out!", an' he locks the door. An' that's the way it's been for two days. He won't open it for Miss Scarlett or anybody, an' he won't say nothin' about the funeral. You've got to help us, he'll listen to you.'

The thought of arguing with Captain Butler while he was half-crazy with sadness made Melanie go cold, but she followed Mammy to Scarlett's house and went quickly up the stairs.

'Please let me come in, Captain Butler,' she said, softly. 'It's Mrs Wilkes. I want to see Bonnie.'

The door opened and Mammy smelled brandy on Rhett's breath as he took Melanie's arm and pulled her inside. Then she sat outside, crying and praying.

After a long, long time, the door opened and Melanie's head appeared. She looked tired, and there were tears in her eyes. 'Go and tell Miss Scarlett that Captain Butler is willing to have the funeral tomorrow morning,' she said.

After Bonnie died, Rhett did not often come home. But when he did, he was usually drunk. Scarlett could not be angry with him, or blame him for Bonnie's death any more. Nothing seemed to matter to her now. She was lonely and unhappy and afraid. There was no one to talk to. Even Mammy had gone back to Tara.

'He loved that child,' Dr Meade told her, 'and he drinks to forget her. Have another baby as quickly as you can.'

But Rhett did not seem to want any more children. He never came to her bedroom, even though she left the door open now.

♦

Scarlett was away from Atlanta for a few days when Rhett's message came: *'Mrs Wilkes is ill. Come home immediately.'*

Rhett was waiting for her at the station with the carriage.

'She's dying, and she wants to see you,' he said.

'Not Melanie! Oh, not Melanie! What happened?'

'She lost the baby she was going to have,' said Rhett.

'I didn't know she was going to have a baby!'

'She didn't tell anyone,' he said.

'Dr Meade said it would kill her to have another baby.'

'It has killed her,' said Rhett.

'But, Rhett, she can't be dying! I didn't when I –'

'She isn't as strong as you,' he said.

The carriage stopped outside Melanie's house.

'Are you coming in?' said Scarlett.

'No,' he said.

She ran inside. Ashley, Aunt Pitty and India were there.

'She asked for you,' Ashley told her.

The door of Melanie's room opened quietly and Dr Meade came out. 'Come with me,' he said to Scarlett. He whispered: 'Miss Melanie is going to die peacefully, and you aren't going to tell her anything about Ashley, do you understand?'

She went into the room where Melanie lay in bed with her eyes closed. Her face was a deathly yellow. Scarlett stared at her – and knew then that Melanie was dying. She had hoped Dr Meade was wrong, but now she knew. '*I need her*!' she thought, and it was true. Suddenly, Scarlett realized how much she needed Melanie – had *always* needed her. Loyal Melanie – who was always there, loving her, fighting for her.

She held Melanie's hand. 'It's me, Melanie,' she said.

Melanie's eyes opened for a second, then they closed again. After a pause, she said 'Promise me?'

'Oh, anything!' cried Scarlett.

'My son – Beau – look after him. I give him to you.'

'I promise,' said Scarlett.

There was a pause before Melanie's whisper came again. 'Ashley,' she said. 'Ashley and you –'

51

Scarlett went cold. Melanie had known all the time! She dropped her head on to the bed and began to cry.

'Ashley,' Melanie said again, and her fingers reached out to touch Scarlett's head. Scarlett looked up into Melanie's eyes – and saw no blame, only the fight for breath to speak.

'Thank God!' she thought. 'She doesn't know!'

'What about Ashley, Melanie?' said Scarlett.

'You'll – look after him,' whispered Melanie.

'Oh, yes,' said Scarlett. 'I'll look after him.'

'But – don't ever let him know.'

'No,' said Scarlett. 'I'll just – suggest things to him.'

Melanie was able to smile.

And so the care of Ashley Wilkes was passed from one woman to another without him ever knowing. But now the fight went out of Melanie's tired face, as if with Scarlett's promise, peace had come to her.

'You're so clever – so brave – always been good to me –'

At these words, it was Scarlett's turn to fight – against the tears that were coming into her eyes. She could not speak.

Dr Meade opened the door, and Scarlett put Melanie's hand against her cheek. 'Good night,' she said.

'Captain Butler –' came the whisper, very softly now. 'Be kind to him. He – loves you so much.'

Then India and Aunt Pitty followed the doctor into the room as Scarlett went outside. 'She was the only woman except Mother who ever loved me,' thought Scarlett.

♦

She found Ashley in his room. He looked at her – and she saw fear and confusion in his eyes.

'What will I do?' he said. 'I can't live without her!'

She stared at him, feeling that she understood him for the first time in her life. 'You – really love her, don't you? Oh, you've

52

been a fool, Ashley! Why didn't you see that you only wanted me like – like Rhett wants that Watling woman?' And then she saw the hurt look in his eyes and remembered her promise to Melanie to look after him. 'Forgive me,' she said.

He came to her quickly and his arms went round her.

'Don't cry, my dear,' she said. 'You must be brave.'

A door opened and someone called: 'Ashley! Quick!'

'Hurry!' said Scarlett, and pushed him out of the room.

'I never saw what he *really* was,' she thought. 'Only what I *wanted* him to be. What a fool I've been! Now Melanie is dead, and I've got him to look after, like a child. Oh, if I hadn't promised her, I wouldn't care if I never saw him again!'

Chapter 14   Tomorrow

Home! That was where she wanted to be. Home with Rhett! Rhett, with his strong arms to hold her. Rhett, who loved her! Melanie had known this, and with her last breath had said: 'Be kind to him.'

'I love him,' Scarlett thought. 'I don't know how long I've loved him, but it's true. Rhett's loved me all the time, and I've been so nasty to him. But I'll tell him I've been a fool and he'll understand, he always has.'

She found him in the dining-room at home.

'Is Miss Melanie dead?' he asked.

Scarlett nodded, suddenly afraid that it may be too late.

'She was the only completely kind person I ever knew,' he said. 'A very great lady.' Then his voice changed. 'So that makes it nice for you, doesn't it?'

'Oh, how can you say that!' cried Scarlett, tears coming into her eyes. 'You know how I loved her! And her last words were about you.'

He came to her quickly and his arms went round her.
'Don't cry, my dear,' she said. 'You must be brave.'

He looked at her. 'What did she say?'

'Oh, not now, Rhett.'

'Tell me,' he said. His voice was cool but the hand he put on her wrist hurt.

'She said – "Be kind to Captain Butler, he loves you so much,"' Scarlett told him.

He stared at her and dropped her wrist. Suddenly he walked across to the window. 'Is that all she said?'

'She said – Ashley – she asked me to look after Ashley.'

He was silent for a moment and then he laughed softly. 'How nice for you,' he said. 'Miss Melanie is dead and you can leave me and go to Ashley, and all your dreams can come true.'

'Leave you?' she cried. 'No! No!' She ran to him and held his arm. 'Oh, you're wrong! I don't want to leave you, I –' She stopped, unable to find the right words.

'You're tired,' he said. 'You'd better go to bed.'

'But I must tell you!' she cried.

'Scarlett,' he said heavily, 'I don't want to hear.'

'But you don't know what I am going to say!'

'My dear, it's written plainly on your face,' he said. 'Something made you realize that you don't love the unfortunate Mr Wilkes after all. And that same something made me seem more attractive suddenly.' He shook his head. 'But it's useless to talk about it.'

'But, Rhett!' she said. 'Oh, I love you so much! I was a fool not to know it! Rhett, you must believe me!'

'Oh, I believe you,' he said. 'And did you ever know that I loved you as much as a man can love a woman? But I couldn't let you know it. You're so cruel to those who love you, Scarlett. I knew you didn't love me when you married me, but I was a fool and thought I could make you care. I wanted to make you happy – the way I made Bonnie happy. But there was always Ashley. Every night I sat across the table from you, and knew that you were wishing Ashley was sitting in my place. But then Bonnie came, and she was like you – brave and pretty and full of life – and I gave her the love that you didn't want. But when she died . . . she took everything.'

'Rhett, there can be other babies –'

'Thank you, no,' he said.

'But Rhett –'

'I'm going away,' he said. 'I'll come back often enough to stop people saying that your husband has left you, if that worries you, but I'm going away.'

'Let me come with you!'

'No,' he said.

'Where – where will you go?' she said.

'Perhaps to England – or Paris.'

'But, if you go – what will I do?' she cried.

He looked at her, and there was pity in his eyes. 'My dear,' he said, softly, 'I don't care what you do.'

She watched him go out of the room and knew that he was the last thing in her world that mattered. She had never understood either him or Ashley, the two men she had loved, and now she had lost them both.

'I won't think of it now,' she told herself. 'I'll go crazy if I think of it now.'

She tried to find some way of stopping the pain.

'I'll – I'll go home to Tara tomorrow!' she thought. 'Yes!'

Tara! She could see the white house, waiting to welcome her through the red autumn leaves. She could see the red earth of the fields and the dark beauty of the trees on the hills.

And Mammy would be there! Suddenly, she wanted Mammy the way she had wanted her when she was a little girl.

Scarlett lifted her chin. She could get Rhett back. There was no man she couldn't get if she really wanted him.

'I'll think of it tomorrow, at Tara,' she told herself. 'Because tomorrow is another day.'

ACTIVITIES

Chapters 1–3

Before you read

1 Look at the picture on page 3. How have things changed at Tara? Do you think Scarlett's life has become easier or more difficult since the war ended?

2 Check these words in your dictionary:

honour   oath   will (n)

  a Add one of these words to the group below and then make a sentence using all the words in the group:

  relatives/money/property/ . . . . .

  b Now put the other two words into this sentence:

  He was a man of . . . . . and she knew he would not break the . . . . . he had taken.

After you read

3 Who in these chapters says:

  a 'There's nothing left for me to fight for.'

  b 'I came here to offer to buy this place, but I won't give you a dollar now!'

  c 'I ain't never seen hair that colour in my life!'

  d 'Sometimes they kill them and leave them with the Ku-Klux card on them.'

  e 'The Yankees think I ran away with the Confederacy gold.'

4 Why does Scarlett go to see Rhett in prison?

5 How does he know she is telling him lies?

Chapters 4–6

Before you read

6 How do you think Rhett can become free again?

7 Will Scarlett get the money she needs from Rhett? How?

8 Find these words in your dictionary:

candle   funeral   fussy   owe   rape   sawmill

Which word means:

a difficult to please when there is a choice to make

b a violent sexual crime against a woman

c a place where trees are cut into smooth pieces for building

d a type of light, before electricity

9 Add one of the words to each of these groups:

a dead/church/family/ . . . . .

b money/pay/financial/ . . . . .

After you read

10 Answer these questions:

a Why does Scarlett become interested in Frank Kennedy?

b What lies does Scarlett tell Frank?

c How much money do the people of Atlanta owe Frank?

d Where is Rhett's money?

e Why is Tony Fontaine running away from Jonesboro?

f What is Scarlett doing that shocks the people of Atlanta?

g Why has Ashley decided to take the job in New York?

11 Do you think Suellen was right to try to make her father take the Yankee Oath? Was it just 'a small lie', as Scarlett believes? Discuss this with other students.

Chapters 7–8

Before you read

12 Do you think Scarlett will keep her promise to Ashley?

13 How do you think Rhett will behave when he knows Scarlett has made Ashley a half-owner in the sawmill?

14 Check these words in your dictionary:

arrest   convict

Write a sentence using both words.

After you read

15 What does Archie tell Scarlett about his past life?

16 Explain Rhett's words: 'Ashley is like a fish out of water.'

17 Why does Scarlett arrange to send Sam back to Tara?

18 Where do these things happen?

    a Scarlett meets Big Sam again.

    b Frank and Ashley meet with the Ku-Klux-Klan.

    c Melanie cuts off Ashley's shirt.

Chapters 9–11

Before you read

19 Do you think there will be more trouble for Ashley because of the Ku-Klux-Klan? What do you think will happen?

20 What will Scarlett do now that Frank is dead?

21 Make sure you understand the word *brandy*, then use it in a sentence with these words: pub/drunk/taxi

After you read

22 Are these sentences true or not true? Correct the sentences that are not true.

    a Rhett notices that Scarlett has been drinking a lot of brandy.

    b Scarlett doesn't want to marry Rhett because she doesn't love him.

    c Scarlett asks Rhett to bring her back a big diamond ring.

    d Scarlett is unhappy when she learns she is going to have another baby.

23 After Archie and India see Ashley and Scarlett together in the office, they go to Melanie's house and tell her about it.

    Student A: You are India

    Student B: You are Archie

    Student C: You are Melanie

    Act out their conversation.

Chapters 12–14

Before you read

24 Do you think Rhett and Scarlett can be happy now? Why or why not?

After you read

25 What is Rhett and Melanie's secret?
26 Why does Scarlett suddenly remember her father?
27 Why is Bonnie's funeral almost delayed?
28 When does Scarlett realize how much she needs Melanie?
29 When does Scarlett realize she loves Rhett?
30 What are Scarlett's plans for the future?

Writing

30 Imagine you are Melanie. Write your diary for the day of Ashley's surprise birthday party.
31 You are a reporter working for an Atlanta newspaper. Write a short report about Bonnie's riding accident.
32 Although Rhett and Scarlett love each other, nothing good comes of their relationship. Who is to blame for this? Could they ever be happy?
33 It is six months after the end of the book. What do you think has happened to Scarlett, Rhett and Ashley in that time? Write a new ending to the story.
34 Did you enjoy *Gone with the Wind*? Write a short report for somebody who has not read the book.
35 Why do you think *Gone with the Wind* was so popular when it first appeared? Why is it still popular? What makes this book special?

Answers for the activities in this book are available from your local
Pearson Education office or contact: Penguin Readers Marketing Department,
Pearson Education, Edinburgh Gate, Harlow, Essex, CM20 2JE.